MW00764292

Ring Tail Raffi

Ring Tail Raffi

MINDFULNESS IN MADAGASCAR

WRITTEN BY SHARI LAROSA

ILLUSTRATIONS BY ALESSANDRA CIMATORIBUS

gatekeeper press
Columbus, Ohio

Ring Tail Raffi: Mindfulness in Madagascar

Published by Gatekeeper Press
2167 Stringtown Rd, Suite 109
Columbus, OH 43123-2989
www.GatekeeperPress.com

Copyright © 2021 by Shari LaRosa
All rights reserved. Neither this book, nor any parts within it may be sold or reproduced in any form or by any electronic or mechanical means, including information storage and retrieval systems, without permission in writing from the author. The only exception is by a reviewer, who may quote short excerpts in a review.

Library of Congress Control Number: 2021938468

ISBN (hardcover): 9781662913471
ISBN (paperback): 9781662913488
eISBN: 9781662913495

The views and opinions expressed in this book are solely those of the author and do not reflect the views or opinions of Gatekeeper Press. Gatekeeper Press is not to be held responsible for and expressly disclaims responsibility of the content herein.

This book is designed to provide helpful information on the subjects discussed. The author does not intend the contents to be a substitute for diagnosis, treatment of medical conditions, or the medical advice of a licensed physician. No expressed or implied guarantee of the effects of the use of the recommendations can be given or liability taken.

Preface

Anxiety is the most common mental health problem in children and adolescents. I began drafting this book in the fall of 2020, after noticing that anxiety had become especially heightened.

It has also been my perception that both children and adults often have difficulty conveying their feelings of anxiety and may present with reactive behavior. It is important to feel safe to express your feelings and emotions. My hope is that this book can help facilitate conversations about anxious feelings between children and adolescents and their parents, mentors, teachers, therapists, or other caregivers in their lives.

In addition, the concept of mindfulness is not often introduced to young minds. As a therapist, I am often first introducing mindfulness concepts and techniques to adults struggling with intrusive anxious thoughts. Why not introduce mindfulness when children are young and provide them with skills to handle various levels of stress affecting their lives?

My inspiration for writing about the ring-tailed lemur came about after a most incredible, interactive, and educational experience I had with lemurs. I came to appreciate these wonderful and interesting animals. Ring Tail Raffi's experience learning about mindfulness in Madagascar aims to highlight the importance of mental health, reduce the stigma surrounding anxiety, and recognize how seeking help when needed can result in learning invaluable skills.

Shari LaRosa

In my world of lush green forests and rain,
all sorts of things happen in my mysterious brain.

I am a lemur, you see - Ring Tail Raffi is me.
I live with my *troop* in my family tree.

Our leader Melala - she's certainly the boss.
She keeps us in line and can become very cross.

We are bouncy, lively, and full of zest.
Yet lately, I haven't been doing my best.

I find that I worry and imagine in my head.
I fear the past and future with dread.

My fur has been itchy and I'm *anxiously* yawning.
Unable to sleep, I'm on guard until morning.

Many *allies* in the wild do help us *thrive*,
yet I tremble at the thought that the *Fossa* might arrive!

I've seen it once before and I've heard the growl.
I've held my ears to mute the howl.
When the Malagasy White Eye and the Flufftail birds flutter away,
they leave us in slumber, *endangered*, a silver platter of *prey*.

I must go seek the wise one, the Red Owl of the Blue Ombre Cave.
She's known to be calm and at ease, and many she has saved.

So I'm setting out on a journey to seek her flight,
with nervous jitters and throat so tight.
My rings of black with ghostly white,
swiftly gliding the trees at remarkable height.

The birch, bamboo, the maple, the oak,
I whiz by the Gecko as Tomato Frogs croak.
Branches and moss vines swing hand over hand,
as I seek the mysterious, magical Red Owl of the land.

Suddenly I stop and see a shimmery glow,
the moonlight reflecting on a wing of yellow.
It's a Comet Moth, oh yes! Her flight can serve well.
"Might you guide me to where the Red Owl does dwell?"

"I would love to help! I know a few ways,
but we must travel fast! I live only four days."
So I take a deep breath with a nervous swallow,
off we go and her lead I follow.

We are making good time and covering ground,
when sudden danger is woven all around.
"Help me, my friend, I'm totally stuck!
This is very rotten bad luck!"

I pause for a moment, then say with a smile,
"For me this is food, once in a while.
I love to eat webs! It's a snack I adore.
I will get you unstuck - I can eat it for sure!

This is a good time to break for a snack.
I will consume this web before the Bark Spider comes back.
I'll gobble each strand and nibble around you with care,
then off we'll go and escape from this scare!"

"This way!" Comet says, "We'll turn left and fly lower."
But suddenly we come upon a sleeping Tree Boa.
Close enough to strike and curled on the limb,
we scurry with hurry or fate will be grim.

A little further to go before we're out of harm's way.
We should be at the cave by the end of the day.
As the sun is coming up, we hop over some logs,
avoiding a pair of poisonous Dart Frogs.

After a day more of travel, we finally arrive
by the rocks at the bottom of the mountainside.
"Here up above is the mouth of the cave.
I'll escort you there, then goodbye I will wave!"

I am so *grateful* for Comet. I wish she could stay.
I'll forever remember how she went out of her way.

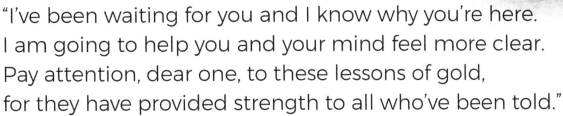

"I've been waiting for you and I know why you're here.
I am going to help you and your mind feel more clear.
Pay attention, dear one, to these lessons of gold,
for they have provided strength to all who've been told."

"We will return you home, that I certainly vow,
and we will start by living in the now.
Let's leave the stress of the past in the past,
and not set our minds on tomorrow too fast."

"Let's stay in the moment we presently are,
look up to the sky, look up to the star.
Slow your breath, count to four, as you gently inhale.
Feel the calm flow, from your head to your tail."

"Exhale for four . . . nice and slow.
I hope you feel more ready to go.
Rise up, my young one. We will travel with care.
In nature we must remain fully aware."

"As a lemur you have magic senses so strong.
You must use your awareness you've had all along.
Be open to the scents, the sounds, and the sights.
Name them aloud and you'll *minimize* your frights."

I see a Giraffe Weevil and a Coua,
I hear   songs
of the Rock Thrush birds
and the distant waterfall.
I smell the fruit, the   and   wild

"When you're feeling worried to a high degree,
imagine where you would like to be.
Where do you feel most at ease?
Might it be high up in the trees?"

"As we move through the forest, don't let it be a *blur*.
Note how you feel in your mind and how you feel in your fur."

"But what if the thought of the *fossa* makes me want to cry?"
"Watch the thought float away like the clouds in the lowland sky!"
"But what if I stay awake all night until the morning birds?"
"Then you will recite these very important words:

I am calm and brave.
I do my very best.
I deserve a peaceful sleep.
I will get plenty of rest.
I am loved, and I do not fear a howl.
I am grateful for my friend
the Wise Red Owl."

Still and steady with no more "I can'ts,"
we soar and pass over the deadly Fire Ants.
So many animal *shrills*, I use my skills -
I breathe in for four and exhale some more.

"One last lesson today to learn.
We will do a Tree Pose by the Fern.
I am calm and balanced deep in my roots.
I am strong and centered," the Red Owl hoots.

The rest of the voyage, traveling side by side,
I review all this knowledge from my feathery guide.

When feeling *anxiety*, any hour,
we can take away its power.
Allow it to rise, fall, and pass through,
it will not remain stuck inside of you.

We glide with intention to arrive before night -
mind, body, and spirit, feeling exceptionally light.

Filled with joy upon returning to the site of my troop,
incredibly tired, my eyelids droop.
With my new sense of calm, I am ready for bed.
I am here in the moment with no sense of dread.

I have learned to let go of the worried thoughts I think.

And the Red Owl flies away with a wink!

Discussion Questions

Why is the Red Owl stressing the importance of staying in the moment?

Did Ring Tail Raffi have any physical symptoms from his anxiety? How did it make his body feel?

What are some examples of Ring Tail Raffi displaying braveness?

What are some examples of acts of kindness in this story?

Why was Raffi grateful for the Comet Moth and the Red Owl?

What are five senses we can engage in to feel grounded and reduce feelings of worry, anxiety, or really big emotions?

An affirmation is a positive statement that helps train our minds to challenge and overcome negative thoughts. Did the Red Owl teach Raffi some affirmations?

What kind of body movement did the Red Owl encourage?

Why is it important for young people to open up about their feelings?

Do we have the power to ease symptoms of stress, worry, fear, and anxiety?

What are some calming skills you learned in this story?

Glossary

Affirmations - positive statements that help train our minds to challenge and overcome negative thoughts.

Allies – others you can trust who are on your side; those who will act and protect each other.

Arboreal – living in trees.

Anxious – experiencing worry; uneasiness of the mind; nervousness.

Blur – unable to be seen clearly.

Carnivorous – feeds on other animals.

Endangered – seriously at risk of extinction; when a species or animal dies out and is gone forever.

Endemic – native and found only in a certain place.

Fossa – the largest carnivorous mammal endemic to the island of Madagascar. They look like a cross between a cat, dog, and mongoose.

Grateful – feeling or showing an appreciation of kindness.

Habitat – the natural home or environment of a plant or animal.

Lemur – an arboreal primate with a pointed snout, large eyes, and long tail, endemic to Madagascar.

Mindfulness – a mental state achieved by focusing one's awareness on the present moment, while calmly accepting and being aware of one's thoughts, feelings, and sensations within one's body.

Minimize – to reduce to the smallest possible amount.

Prey – an animal that is hunted and killed by another for food.

Shrills – piercing high-pitched sounds.

Thrive – to grow or develop well; to prosper or flourish.

Troop – a group.

Fun facts

Ring-tailed lemurs are *endemic* to Madagascar, an island off the east coast of Africa. They live in the rainforest as well as some of the dry spiny forest areas.

Ring-tailed lemurs live in groups known as troops, which may include six to thirty lemurs, but on average about seventeen. Both males and females live in the troops; however, a dominant female presides over all troop members.

Ring-tailed lemurs spend much time on the ground and walk on all fours.

Ring-tailed lemurs will often groom themselves and others using their front bottom teeth, which form a comb-like structure they can run through their fur.

When a lemur yawns, it can be related to their anxiety level. They will yawn more frequently after being threatened by a predator.

Fruit makes up a large part of the ring-tailed lemur diet, but they also eat leaves, flowers, tree bark, sap, and of course enjoy a good spider web!

You can often find ring-tailed lemurs sun-bathing with outstretched arms, in yoga-like poses, on the ground and in the trees. They like to warm themselves up in the mornings with their arms outstretched, like they are welcoming the world!

Ring-tailed lemurs can live for up to fifteen years in the wild.

The ring-tailed lemur's tail is longer than its body!

The ring-tailed lemur is known as *maki* in Malagasy, the language spoken in Madagascar.

The ring-tailed lemur's Latin name is *catta* because of its cat-like looks.

Male ring-tailed lemurs have scent glands on their wrists and shoulders. They will pull their tails through these glands and wave them at rivals. It is known as "stink fighting"!

Lemurs are prosimians, which literally means "before monkeys."

Ring-tailed lemurs usually have just one baby at a time, although they can have twins. Mothers carry their babies on their fronts for the first couple of weeks and then on their backs when the babies are a bit stronger.

The Comet Moth is also native to the rainforests of Madagascar. The adult moth cannot feed and lives only four or five days.

Concerning fact

Lemurs are the most *endangered* animals on the planet. One third of all lemurs are critically endangered (according to the IUCN Red List of Threatened Species) with 96 percent threatened with extinction due to habitat loss, hunting, and the pet trade.

ABOUT THE AUTHOR

Shari LaRosa is a licensed clinical therapist, a proud wife, and mom to two college-age daughters. With an additional degree in elementary education, Shari blends her passion for helping others, experience teaching children, and love of animals and nature to expose young readers to mindful awareness in a creative fashion. She hopes to encourage open dialogue about anxiety so when children recognize symptoms of worry, there is greater comfort in disclosing their feelings with others they trust. Shari is a specialist in treating anxiety and works with teens and adults of all ages in her private practice, *Connected Mind Counseling*.

Lightning Source UK Ltd.
Milton Keynes UK
UKHW021031011221
394864UK00003B/60

9 781662 913488